MR SPARKS
TO THE RESCUE

First published in Great Britain by HarperCollins Publishers Ltd in 1997

3 5 7 9 10 8 6 4

Copyright © 1997 Enid Blyton Company Ltd. Enid Blyton's
signature mark is a Registered Trade Mark of Enid Blyton Ltd.

ISBN: 0 00 172013 9

Story by Fiona Cummings
Cover design and illustrations by County Studios
A CIP catalogue for this title is available from the British Library.

Printed and bound in Singapore.

Enid Blyton™

TOYLAND™ STORIES

MR SPARKS
TO THE RESCUE

Collins

An Imprint of HarperCollins*Publishers*

It was a very exciting day for Mr Sparks. He had a new car wash at the garage.

"I'll just check that everything works," he said to himself proudly.

He turned on the tap. He could hear a nice **gurgle, gurgle** inside the hose.

Then he went to the other end of the hose.

"That's funny," he said, as he lifted the hose.

"Where is the water?"

But at that very moment the water started to gush out, *SQUIRTING* him in the face.

"Ah, it works perfectly!" Mr Sparks said with delight. "All I need now are some customers!"

It was not very long before Mr Sparks heard a PARP, PARP coming in his direction.

"Ah," he said to himself with a smile. "That must be Noddy's car!"

Mr Sparks was hoping that Noddy's car would not be very clean. He was in luck. As the little car came into view, Mr Sparks saw that it was not quite as shiny as usual.

"Hello Noddy!" Mr Sparks called. "Would you like to try my brand new car washing service? It will make your car nice and clean again."

"Will it?" Noddy asked eagerly. "I've been so busy giving people rides this morning that I haven't had time to clean it myself."

"It will only take five minutes," Mr Sparks said. "Just jump out of your car and I'll switch on my special hose."

So Noddy switched off his engine while Mr Sparks went into the garage to turn on the tap. But just then, it started to rain *very* heavily!

"I won't be needing your car wash after all,
Mr Sparks," Noddy called. "My car will get clean in
the rain!" And at that Noddy turned on his engine.

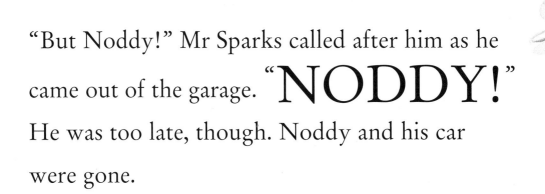

"But Noddy!" Mr Sparks called after him as he came out of the garage. "NODDY!" He was too late, though. Noddy and his car were gone.

"Well, I can't blame him," Mr Sparks muttered to himself. "Who wants a car wash in the rain? I'll just have to hope that the rain soon stops."

But the rain did not stop. It just became heavier and heavier. Poor Mr Sparks. His new car wash was not going to be busy today!

"Perhaps I'll have more luck with my breakdown truck," Mr Sparks said to himself. "I'll drive it around Toy Town and see if anyone needs help."

But Mr Sparks was not lucky with his breakdown truck either. He drove it all the way to the harbour and all the way back again but he did not meet one car. Where was everyone?

"I suppose no one wants to go out in heavy rain like this," he grumbled. "What a miserable day I'm having!"

Mr Sparks was not the only one
who was having a miserable day.

Noddy was too. He suddenly appeared at Mr Sparks' garage. And he was *very* wet and *very* cross.

"Mr Sparks, you must help me," he said. "After I left you, I drove to Big-Ears' house to see if I could borrow an umbrella."

"Very wise with all the rain, Noddy," Mr Sparks said. Then he lifted his hat to scratch his head.

"But where is the umbrella, Noddy? You're as wet as a fish!"

"I never reached Big-Ears' house," Noddy explained.

"The rain had made it so muddy in the Dark Wood that my car got stuck. I need your breakdown truck to pull it out!"

Mr Sparks was delighted to be able to help.
"Just wait here, Noddy. I'll fetch the truck."

Soon they were ready to set off.

"Don't worry, Noddy, we'll be at the Dark Wood in a flash!" said Mr Sparks.

And in a flash they were. Noddy's car looked such a sorry sight stuck in the mud. The mud came halfway up the tyres!

"Never mind, Noddy," said Mr Sparks. "My truck will soon pull your car out."

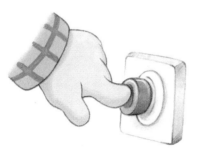

Mr Sparks pressed a special button in his truck so that the big hook at the back started to come down.

When it was low enough, Mr Sparks attached it to Noddy's car.

Mr Sparks then sat in his truck and started the engine. He made the engine go a bit faster, then a bit faster. At first nothing happened. But then it started to move forward very slowly.

And Noddy's car started to move as well!

"Oh thank you, Mr Sparks, thank you!" Noddy
cried. "My car isn't stuck any more!"

Mr Sparks was also delighted. He loved using his breakdown truck. And this was not the only business he would be doing today. Noddy's car now needed a very good clean... and this time there was no rain to do the job.

"It looks as if you'll have to use my new car wash after all, Noddy!" Mr Sparks chuckled.

THE NODDY CLASSIC LIBRARY
by Enid Blyton ™

1. NODDY GOES TO TOYLAND
2. HURRAH FOR LITTLE NODDY
3. NODDY AND HIS CAR
4. HERE COMES NODDY AGAIN!
5. WELL DONE NODDY!
6. NODDY GOES TO SCHOOL
7. NODDY AT THE SEASIDE
8. NODDY GETS INTO TROUBLE
9. NODDY AND THE MAGIC RULER
10. YOU FUNNY LITTLE NODDY
11. NODDY MEETS FATHER CHRISTMAS
12. NODDY AND TESSIE BEAR
13. BE BRAVE LITTLE NODDY!
14. NODDY AND THE BUMPY-DOG
15. DO LOOK OUT NODDY!
16. YOU'RE A GOOD FRIEND NODDY!
17. NODDY HAS AN ADVENTURE
18. NODDY GOES TO SEA
19. NODDY AND THE BUNKY
20. CHEER UP LITTLE NODDY!
21. NODDY GOES TO THE FAIR
22. MR PLOD AND LITTLE NODDY
23. NODDY AND THE TOOTLES
24. NODDY AND THE AEROPLANE

Available in hardback
Published by HarperCollins